WHAT'S SILLY HAIR DAY WITH NO HAIR?

Norene Paulson

illustrated by Camila Carrossine

Albert Whitman & Company
Chicago, Illinois

Bea wore hats everywhere.

Sometimes Bea's best friend, Shaleah, wore hats too.

But Bea never worried about "hat hair" like Shaleah because under Bea's hats...

there was no hair.
Bea had hair when she was born. A lot of hair.
But...

Before Bea turned four, she was bald.
Would her hair grow back? No one knew.

Bea couldn't remember having hair, so most days she didn't think about being bald.
Her family loved her.

Her friends didn't care,
and when people stared,
Bea just smiled.

But some days being bald was all she thought about.
Like when Shaleah got new hair clips, and Bea wished she
could borrow them.

Or when a classmate called her a mean name.

Or when everyone was excited about Silly Spirit Week.
Everyone but Bea.

"One of the days is Silly Hair Day? What about me?"
Bea yanked off her hat.

"We'll think of something," said Shaleah.

SILLY SPIRIT WEEK

MONDAY – SILLY COSTUME DAY
TUESDAY – SILLY BACKWARDS DAY
WEDNESDAY – SILLY HAT DAY
THURSDAY – SILLY FEET DAY
FRIDAY – SILLY HAIR DAY

Bea wasn't so sure.

On Saturday Shaleah suggested a silly wig, so Bea's mom
took them to Characters-to-Go.

Bea tried on long wigs,

short wigs,

and way-too-big wigs.

"It's like a hat with hair," said Shaleah.

But the hair fell in Bea's eyes,
itched her scalp,
and tickled her neck.
Silly? Yes, thought Bea. *But right?*
Not quite.

On Sunday the girls tried crafting some silly hair.
They cut and glued.
And clipped and braided.
"THIS is it!" said Shaleah.

Silly? Yes, thought Bea. *But right?*
Not quite.

"Looks like a nest of gummy worms," said Bea, flinging the cap in the trash. "This wouldn't be so hard if I just...HAD...HAIR! Maybe I should stay home on Friday."

"But you'd miss the Silly Spirit Week picnic," said Shaleah.

When Bea shrugged, Shaleah added, "If you stay home, I stay home."

"Then YOU'LL miss the picnic!" Bea sighed. "I'll think of something."

But would she?

On Monday Bea had superpowers for Silly Costume Day but...
no idea for Silly Hair Day.
And she only had three days to think of something.

On Tuesday Bea rocked Silly Backwards Day but...
still no idea for Silly Hair Day.
Her stomach fluttered.

SILLY SPIRIT WEEK

MONDAY - SILLY COSTUME DAY

TUESDAY - SILLY BACKWARDS DAY

WEDNESDAY - SILLY HAT DAY

THURSDAY - SILLY FEET DAY

FRIDAY - SILLY HAIR DAY

On Wednesday Bea won the Wackiest Hat Award but...
an idea for Silly Hair Day? Nope.
Now her stomach started flip-flopping. Only one more
day to think of something.

Then during lunch on Silly Feet Day—
an idea!
Silly? Yes, thought Bea. *But right?*
Not quite...

UNLESS Shaleah and Ms. Chambers agreed.
Bea asked Shaleah first...Yes!

During recess the girls headed to Ms. Chambers's
office. High fives!
Silly? Yes. But right?
Absolutely.

After school Bea and Shaleah went shopping,
rummaged through craft boxes,

searched through junk drawers,
and worked late into the night.

The next morning Bea's mom dropped the girls off early.

One by one students noticed the new sign outside Ms. Chambers's office.

"Silly Hair or HEAD day?" questioned one classmate.

"What? Why?" asked another.

SILLY SPIRIT WEEK

FRIDAY
SILLY
HAIR OR HEAD
DAY

Bea slowly lowered her hood.

"Because now…"

"Everyone can participate!"
Bea and Shaleah said together.

Their classmates marveled at the silly gem
and tattoo designs on the girls' heads.
Bea and Shaleah grinned at each other.
Silly? Yes. And just right.

Hair Loss in Children

Alopecia is an autoimmune skin disorder that causes hair loss in adults and children, like Bea. There are three types of alopecia. Alopecia areata causes irregular patches of hair loss on the scalp and other areas of the body. Alopecia totalis is the complete loss of all head hair, and Alopecia universalis results in the loss of all body hair. Alopecia affects each person differently and often first appears during childhood. Although it is possible for hair to grow back at any time, there is no guarantee regrowth will happen, and at this time there is no cure.

To learn more about alopecia, visit the websites of the National Alopecia Areata Foundation (naaf.org) and the Children's Alopecia Project (childrensalopeciaproject.org).

Another reason for hair loss is cancer treatment. Certain cancer-fighting medicines may cause partial or complete hair loss. Cancer cells divide rapidly. Chemotherapy drugs are designed to attack rapidly dividing cells. However, other normal cells, such as hair cells, also divide rapidly. Some chemo drugs can't tell the difference, so they attack both. The extent of hair loss caused by chemo drugs differs from one patient to the next. Some experience only thinning hair while others experience complete hair loss. Fortunately, regrowth occurs shortly after treatments stop although hair may grow back a slightly different color or texture.

For more information on this and other causes of children's hair loss, visit the American Hair Loss Association's website (americanhairloss.org).

Hey, it's me, Bea—
Thinking about getting some cool temporary tattoos?
If so, here are some important things to remember:

1. When using temporary tattoos, always ask an adult for help, and follow the package directions.

2. You want tattoos that are nontoxic and use certified colorants. Ask an adult to read the labels before buying. Tattoos made in the United States, Canada, and the European Union meet or exceed safety standards.

3. Press-on or water-transfer tattoos are best. Henna-based tattoos could cause an allergic reaction (although that's rare).

To Naomi; thanks for being on this journey with me.—NP

To Luna and Alê, my rosemary and my heart—CC

Library of Congress Cataloging-in-Publication data is on file with the publisher.
Text copyright © 2021 by Norene Paulson
Illustrations copyright © 2021 by Albert Whitman & Company
Illustrations by Camila Carrossine
First published in the United States of America
in 2021 by Albert Whitman & Company
ISBN 978-0-8075-0608-0 (hardcover)
ISBN 978-0-8075-0609-7 (ebook)

Printed in China
10 9 8 7 6 5 4 3 2 1 WKT 24 23 22 21 20

Design by Valerie Hernández

For more information about Albert Whitman & Company,
visit our website at www.albertwhitman.com.